Talon:
An Alien Scifi Romance

DEMELZA CARLTON

ONE

"I understand you have a pest problem," Talon said, leaning against the desk.

The woman behind it jerked back in surprise. "I didn't hear you come in."

Talon gave her a lazy grin. "Owls are known for being silent hunters. That's what makes us the best pest control team in the galaxy, right boys?" He glanced back at the flock of meowls, who only ruffled their feathers and did their best to ignore him. Must be the cat part of their DNA, he decided, because unmodified owls definitely responded to sound.

The woman sniffed, eyeing the chimeras with distaste. She might run a farm, but she was definitely the administration type. She'd probably never picked up a shovel in her life. "I can't see why we need more animals here. Surely we can just put down some poison baits."

Definitely a townie, and a dirtsider at that. Someone who didn't know the first thing about life in space, or under a dome. "Because poisons leach into the soil and the water supply, and you've got to get the pests to eat the poison in the first place. Not to mention poison is a horrific way to die. That's animal cruelty, right there, and against the law here in the Colony." She was Human, then. No Titan could even stand to hear about animal cruelty, let alone suggest it. "Whereas my meowls are experts in aerial search and destroy. Instant death your rats will never see coming. It is rats you have here, am I right?" Talon peered at his tablet, swiping his knuckle across the screen.

"Yes. I don't understand where they came from. The Colony is meant to be a new, clean city, with no vermin at all."

"Just like every colony in the history of colonies. Where there are people, there are rats. They stow away on ships and pop up where and when you least expect them. And when they do, you call me, and I bring my crew to take care of it for you."

The woman pursed her lips, as if she was about to change her mind about hiring him. If she tried, she was about to find out she didn't have a choice. He owned every meowl in the Colony.

"Seeing as you know so much about colonies, Mr Talon, I'm sure you will understand that every colony also has its precious young women, who are the real future of the Colony. Star Farm is a school, a very exclusive school for young women, specially selected for both their genetic profile and their ability to learn, as our FarmStars, as we called them back on Earth, will be the key to terraforming Elysium. But until they are ready, Star

Farm is the sanctuary where we keep them safe. In fact, most of our girls have never seen an alien, and I would like to keep it so for as long as possible. Therefore, you will avoid all contact with them, only working at night when the girls have gone to bed, and should you encounter one of the girls, you will not speak a word to them. Those are the rules here at Star Farm. Do you think you can follow them, Mr Talon?" Her eyes glittered dangerously.

"Or what? You'll spank me?" he asked.

Laughter should not sound that dark. "Oh, I do not think it will come to that, Mr Talon. Unless that is where your tastes lie, in which case…perhaps we can consider that a reward in lieu of a bonus, if you can manage to follow the rules and rid the farm of vermin."

Being spanked by an old lady. He'd seen a lot of horror films in his time, but the image this conjured up had to be worse than all the films combined. Talon couldn't suppress a shudder. "No, thanks. My terms are payment in cold, hard credits only. We'll do the job, you'll pay the bill, and everyone will be happy."

"If you're sure…"

Stars, yes. "Absolutely. Can you show me where we can set up?"

A sharp nod. "Of course. If you'll just follow…" Her tablet beeped to indicate in incoming call. Her eyes widened. "I have to take this. I'll get one of the girls to show you." She stuck her head out of the office and shouted, "Rue! Rue! Come here right now!"

TWO

Rue finished wiping down the last table, and breathed a sigh of relief that her punishment detail was finally over. For a pack of girls eating supposedly low-mess protein bars, there sure were a lot of crumbs to clean up. Evidently she wasn't the only one who hated the taste and texture of them, but just because she'd been the only one to actually say something about how odd it was that the girls actually growing food had to eat this shit when they could be eating fresh produce at every meal…

"Rue! Rue! Come here right now!"

Rue bit back the retort she wanted to make to Donna and pasted a smile on her face. She was not going to clean up the dining hall for another week's worth of punishment. "Yes, Donna?"

"I said come here!"

Rue trudged across the dining room to Donna's office. The moment she stepped inside, her mouth dropped open.

"This is Mr Talon and his crew. They're here to deal with the rats. Please show them to the equipment shed, and then forget all about them. I don't want you to breathe a word about them to any of the other girls."

Rue closed her mouth and marched out again.

"Ah, Mr Falcon, sorry to have kept you waiting," Donna began before the door slammed, narrowly missing the behind of…well, an alien. A whole flock of aliens, riding on the back of a bigger alien the size of a large pony. Every one of them had four legs, wings, and a beak, but that's where the similarities ended, because each had different colours and markings.

"Um, if you'll all come with me, please?" Rue asked, looking from one rider to the other. "Which one of you is in charge?" Damn it, she'd been so busy staring at the aliens, she'd forgotten his name.

The largest alien, which she'd taken for a sort of flying horse, unfolded one wing and raised it like she might raise her hand in class.

"Oh." She swallowed. "I'm sorry, I've never seen an alien before."

The big one rolled his eyes.

He must think she was an absolute bloody idiot. Like it was her fault she'd slept through the war in stasis, only to wake up here on Star Farm inside the Colony, instead of Elysium, where she was supposed to be. The only reason Donna had been able to give for the change was the dangerous aliens they were now forced to share a system and the city with. Dangerous aliens like this one.

She slowed her steps so that she could walk beside him, and take a closer look at him.

He had a face like a white owl, complete with beak, but on a much bigger scale than any owl she'd seen at home. Unlike an owl, he had four legs instead of two, but each pair was as different as her hands and feet. His hands, if you could call them that, were more like talons, tipped with wickedly long claws that she imagined would be terribly sharp. His feet resembled the hind paws of a very large cat, though she'd never seen a cat with paws bigger than her own feet before. While they looked soft and fluffy, she didn't doubt those hid claws just as deadly as the ones on his hands.

He had white wings on his back, too, covered in dark grey spots. Actually, most of him was covered in dark grey spots, from the crown of his head all the way along to his…

Rue just couldn't help herself. She let out a squeal.

THREE

"Oh my God, I love your tail!"

Before Talon could react, she'd grabbed it in both hands and began rubbing it against her cheek.

"Oh, it's so soft and fluffy. I've never felt anything like it. Ohh, I love it!"

Between the blissful look on her face and the old woman's warning not to speak to the girl, Talon couldn't bring himself to tell her to let go of his tail. In all fairness, the girl wasn't hurting him — he could tolerate a bit of soft rubbing and stroking. He couldn't remember the last time anyone had done either of those things. Definitely not a child like this one, filled with such innocence that just this simple touch brought her so much joy.

She seemed to sense him staring at her. She flushed and released his tail. "Sorry. You have the most incredible, irresistible tail. I should…show you the equipment shed and let you get to work."

Talon nodded. He wanted to smile at her, to tell her it was all right, but beaks didn't really smile and as for telling her anything…instead, he just sighed and followed her.

"You think I'm just a kid, don't you? It's because I'm small, I know. I'm not, though. I'm actually the oldest girl here. I was twenty-one last birthday. Iva's the youngest, and she turns eighteen next week. That means she was fifteen when she signed up for the FarmStars program, so she must have lied about her age on the application, because they only wanted girls who were between sixteen and eighteen. I signed the contracts the day before my eighteenth birthday, and our training started the next day. I was surprised at how much there was for even me to learn, and I grew up on a farm. But farming in space is different to farming on Earth…"

She continued to chatter about her training on Earth, which sounded a lot like his university degree in agriculture, only compressed into a much tighter timeframe. Two years instead of four. Yet somehow, her course had included a lot more practical experience than his had. The more she said, the more he wanted to ask her advice about how to better utilise the farming plot he'd been given as meowl habitat.

Except...he couldn't.

It took him a moment to realise she'd fallen silent, her hand pointing at the darkened building ahead.

"That's the smaller of the two equipment sheds, where we keep the stuff we don't use so often. It's actually the hayshed, but because we have so much farming equipment, and not a lot of hay, we store the haymaking gear in here, so it's not in the way the rest of the year. I figured you'd be more comfortable in here with the haybales, than in the actual equipment shed, which is mostly full of machinery. Also, no one's going to come here, so you'll have it all to yourself. If the other girls knew there was an actual alien inside the farm, half of them would come to take a peek at you, while the other half would probably freak out and do something stupid. We've all been warned about how dangerous you are, you see." She grinned.

What was her name again? The old lady had definitely shouted it loud enough. Ruru? He'd always thought that was a boy's name, but she was definitely a girl. Well, a woman, if she truly was twenty-one, like she'd said.

And she was still grinning at him. Like she didn't think he was dangerous at all.

Talon sighed. He marched up to the shed, shoved the sliding door wide enough for him to go inside, and strode into the darkness. The meowls on his back rustled their feathers and clicked their beaks – they could hear the rats rustling in the rafters, and they itched to begin the hunt.

He let out a string of high-pitched chittering punctuated by clicks, telling the meowls to hunt until dawn, bringing back any prey they killed to him here. Of course, because they were meowls, they didn't acknowledge him at all. The moment he was done talking, they scattered.

"Is that your language?"

Of course she was still there, watching.

Talon shook his head and pointed at a meowl who'd decided to go for the easy prey in the rafters. Lothario, of course. He was the laziest of the lot.

"Ohhh, so they're a different species to you? Not just…littler?"

Talon nodded. Even if he was allowed to speak to her, meowls took a lot of explaining, and most people lost interest before he even got to the good parts.

He had to give her credit for choosing a good shed, though. He lifted down several hay bales, pushing them together until he had a surface big enough for a bed, then climbed on top of them and settled in, sphinx style.

"Oh. Um. Is there anything else you need?"

Talon shook his head without opening his eyes.

"Right. Okay. I'll check in with you again in the morning, in case you need anything. Uh, good night and good hunting, I guess."

He inclined his head in thanks, though he suspected it was too dark for her to see. Then she was gone.

FOUR

There was a movie on the screen in the common room, but Rue couldn't hear a word of it over the other girls chattering. Then again, she didn't much care — she wasn't in the mood for an old Earth movie, anyway. On the screen, a bird of prey circled over the desert, reminding her of her parents' farm, the farm that bushfire had turned back to desert, when the flames took everything from her.

Even birds. She couldn't remember the last time she'd seen one, especially one in flight. It must have been back on Earth, probably the day they took the space elevator up to Exodus Space Station to go into stasis on the *Genesis*, the first step in their long journey here. Only to find aliens had arrived first.

Avian aliens. The little ones could fly. She wondered about the big one, the guy in charge. She'd bet he looked majestic, soaring across the skies, with wings wider than a crop duster's. A twinge of sadness twisted in her chest at the thought. Her parents had promised that when the farm was making proper profits, they'd pay for her to get her pilot's licence, and her own plane, so she could handle all the aerial work. If all their plans hadn't gone up in smoke, she'd have them by now.

Instead, she was lightyears away from home, an orphan on a farm in a space colony full of aliens.

She felt the tears well up, and she knew she couldn't hold them back this time.

A hand landed on her arm. "Are you all right?" Franny asked, concerned.

They'd gone to the district high school together – but when Rue had been sent to the agricultural college as a boarder in Year 10, Franny had stayed in town to do her apprenticeship in her mum's bakery. Still, even with the years apart, Franny knew her better than anyone alive.

Rue shook her head. "I might just go to bed early."

Franny nodded. "I'll keep the others here for a while longer, to give you some time to yourself."

Rue hurried out of the common room, just as she heard Franny shout out an offer to paint people's nails. No one turned down one of Franny's manicures or pedicures, because by the time Franny finished, every nail was a work of art.

As the darkness swallowed her, she let the tears fall until her vision blurred and she found herself stumbling blindly through what she thought was the dormitory door.

Only for hay to crunch underfoot as she stepped inside.

FIVE

A small shape stumbled through the doorway, casting a shadow across the floor that reached Talon's hay bale bed. He blinked the sleep from his eyes, rising before whoever it was could say he was sleeping on the job. They'd be right, but it wasn't like the meowls needed to be supervised while they hunted. They were a mix of cat and owl DNA, uniquely crafted to be the apex predator in a space station environment. They were born to hunt, and only by some quirk of his ancestry, he'd been born with the ability to communicate with and command them.

But his visitor definitely wasn't a meowl. If Talon wasn't mistaken, she was drunk.

It took every bit of his self control not to call out, "Can I help you?" He might only be half owl, but he was all stealth hunter, and it was better that the drunk girl realised she'd come to the barn instead of her bedroom, and without knowing he was here.

"I'm sorry," she whispered. "I meant to go to the dormitory, but my feet led me here instead. I was thinking about everything I missed on Earth, and when I felt lonely or upset back home, I'd sneak into the barn. Do you mind?"

Talon found himself shaking his head before his brain caught up, and then it was too late. Ruru – for of course it was her, none of the other girls knew where to find him – sat on the haybale next to his, hugging her knees to her chest with one arm, while wiping her eyes with the sleeve on her other arm.

Not drunk, he realised, as she let out a pathetic sniffle, before drawing in a deep, strengthening breath. She was upset, and that's what had made her stumble. If she was one of his sisters, Bastet or Sekhmet, he'd ask her what was wrong, and who he'd have to kill. Of course, both of his sisters had claws of their own, just as destructive as his talons, and they were more than capable of shredding the flesh of any man stupid enough to wrong them without any help from him. They'd served in the war against Humans for the Altan System, and even now were out patrolling. Unlike him, a glorified ratcatcher all through the war, right up until the present day.

Or night, as it always tended to be in the Nyx Dome.

But no matter how much woolgathering he did, it still wouldn't change the fact that there was an innocent girl sitting beside him in tears that he was powerless to stop. So he extended a wing around her shoulders, and she just sort of fell against him, sobbing.

He'd learned young that if one of his sisters came to him for a hug and a good cry, he'd be risking his life or at the very least a claw to the face if he moved before they were done. Ruru might not have either of his sisters' fighting prowess, but as her story spilled out of her, he could no more let her go than he could make everything go back to the way it was.

She'd grown up on a farm, he learned, which her parents had managed before it had gone up for sale, and they'd bought it, planning to turn it into a vineyard. They'd farmed different things while the grapevines matured enough to yield a decent harvest, as well as providing agistment for rich people's horses.

Taking care of the horses had been her job, before and after school, including exercising them when the rich owners couldn't be bothered coming down to ride them.

A meowl flew in and dropped an eviscerated rat at Talon's feet, then perched on a piece of farm equipment, preening itself.

Talon half expected the girl to run screaming out of the barn, like most of the Human women would do.

Instead, she hopped down from her haybale and nudged the corpse with her shoe. "Fat bastard, isn't it? I wonder what they've been eating to get so fat. I'm sure I'll find out, come harvest, when the yield's down. Not like we can blame drought or poor soil here, where everything's so controlled. I thought we'd be free of pests and diseases out here, though. I mean, the quarantine protocols for the *Genesis* had us in isolation for weeks…"

As she detailed the isolation she and the other girls had endured, it began to dawn on Talon that Ruru's trip to the Altan System had been planned, unlike the Titan refugees or even most of the other Human inhabitants of the system. She'd spent years preparing to come to this place, because she genuinely wanted to be here.

Like the original pioneers who terraformed Tito. That took a crazy amount of courage. The kind of courage this girl had by the bucketload. Stars, she'd picked up the dead rat by the tail, and now she was scrunching her nose up at it.

His sisters would recoil in horror at the thought of even touching a dead rat. Oh, hunting and killing it, they didn't mind, but dealing with the corpse afterwards…

"Will you want them to feed to your team after they're finished, or should I just put the bodies in the recycler?" Ruru asked.

Talon just stared at her. Even if he had an answer for her, he wasn't allowed to tell her. He hadn't even thought about it until now.

Ruru seemed to sense his confusion, almost like she could read his mind. Or maybe just his expression. "Tell you what. I'll grab a bucket, and we can put them all in there. That way, if there are too many for your birds, we can tip what's left into the recycler." Into the bucket went the body, before she strode over to the sink and washed her hands. Then she climbed back onto the haybale beside Talon. "You know, we had a mouse plague once, before Mum and Dad owned the farm, and the owner couldn't be bothered spending the money to get them eradicated properly, especially when the plague wasn't just at our place, it was across the whole district. They got everywhere. I remember Mum ran me a bath once and before the tub was even full, there was one swimming for its life in there. And when I opened the chook food barrel to feed them, the whole thing was just a writhing, wriggling mass of them. Like giant maggots…"

Definitely not like most of the other girls he'd met, Talon decided, as he loafed on his haybale and listened.

SIX

Rue's neck ached, and something scratchy seemed to be trying to sneak down her shirt. It was almost like the time she'd fallen asleep in Sultan's stable, the night before she got sent off to board at the agricultural college. Only this time, the place didn't smell like horse manure.

She opened her eyes and swore. She was in the hayshed. Dawn was working its way through the open door and the alien – who she'd surely spent the night with, sleeping as soundly as she had beside Sultan – along with his entourage of flying owl-like creatures, was gone.

Worse, it sounded like the other girls were awake and already having breakfast, and they were bound to ask questions if she came in late. Questions she didn't want to answer, because without the alien here, no one would believe her.

Swearing under her breath, Rue sneaked into the ordinary equipment shed and pulled out a seeder. She wheeled it out of the shed, heading for the field they were scheduled to sow today.

"Suck up," someone hissed.

Yep, they'd definitely seen her. It was like being back in high school again sometimes. The difference between then and now was that now she knew who she was, and what she wanted…so she didn't care what the others thought of her. She was here to make her parents' dream a reality, even if they weren't around to see it. She wanted a farm of her own, and she intended to devote every waking moment to working out how to make this strange alien planet productive, so that when she had her own farm, she'd know exactly what to do, and how to do it.

She'd heard the others say they wanted the easy way out – they planned to get pregnant as early as possible, and bear the Colony four babies, after which they'd be free of their contract so they wouldn't have to work on the farm any more. Fine by her. She intended to be the last woman standing, so that when all the other girls had left, Donna would have no choice but to appoint her the farm manager, and Rue would have the run of the place. Maybe even be willing to sell her the place at a good price…

Rue sighed as she tore open a sack of seed and started filling the hopper. What she really wanted was a farm on some planet's surface, where she could breathe real, natural air, and stare up at the sky. Not that the sky on any of these planets would look like Earth's, but…

Altan was a red giant, so the ruddy light meant growing specially modified plants that were suited to that kind of low light environment. In one of the scenarios they'd studied during their training, crops would have to be grown under a dome of artificial lighting if they couldn't be adapted to the light of Altan. Not unlike Star Farm here, with the lights all over the ceiling, except with air and rain and weather…

One day, she told herself. One day, she'd live on a farm open to the sky, with birds flying overhead. But first, she had to get this farm producing whatever experimental grain Eden Labs had given them this time. She checked the sack. Rosa Frost 55C Wheat, apparently. She hoped this would be better than the last spindly crop this field had sported. She wasn't sure whether it was the wheat varietal, or the low light that was responsible for the poor harvest, but she'd like to find out. The supply of ration bars had to run out eventually, and they'd need to be producing their own food by then. It wasn't like they could just pop back home to Earth to pick up a loaf of bread.

She'd almost forgotten what bread tasted like. All the more reason to get this wheat sown and growing, so Franny could bake them something worth eating.

Then her foot sank into the ground, almost to the knee. A burrow, which had to belong to one of those…

Something squirmed against her ankle, before the biggest rat she'd ever seen barrelled out of the hole, heading for the other side of the field.

She'd better tell Donna the alien hadn't eradicated them all, then. Rue couldn't help but grin. Then he'd have to come back another night.

SEVEN

Rue hung back after dinner, hoping to see the alien arrive. Not that she'd need to show him to the equipment shed this time — he and his crew already knew where to go.

"What are you doing here?" Donna asked.

Rue managed a smile. "Cleaning up

the crumbs, like you told me to." Her punishment detail had actually finished yesterday.

Donna frowned, as if she knew Rue was lying.

Rue thought desperately of something to say to avoid getting sent to solitary, where she wouldn't be able to see the alien. "I think Dani might be sick. She hasn't finished her ration bars at any meal in the last two days." Sick of eating protein bars, instead of real food, Rue hoped, but if Dani was unwell, she should receive proper medical attention. Even Dani herself would agree. Hell, she'd probably already reported it to Donna, so…

Donna's eyes widened. "We can't allow illness to affect Star Farm. I shall conduct a health check immediately." She managed two strides across the dining room before something chimed in the office behind her. Donna glanced back, indecision clear on her expression. "It can wait until morning," she said, hurrying back into the office.

Rue heard the door shut before she dared to breathe again. It didn't sit well with her to inform on anyone, let alone sunny Dani, who'd actually bought into the working together to build a better world bullshit that had been drilled into them during their training. Well, Dani wasn't alone in wanting a better world, but Rue had no illusions about being the ones who'd live in it. The better world of a terraformed Elysium was a minimum of fifty years away, if not more, and Rue refused to have children unless she knew for certain their children would see that better world.

She'd never thought that world would include aliens.

But watching the alien and his crew pad silently over to the equipment shed, she couldn't bring herself to believe that was a bad thing. Perhaps building a better world meant being more than just Human. Thinking like a galactic citizen, instead of just one world.

She wandered over to the common room, too deep in thought to register what the others were saying or watching, until the lights went out in the dormitory. Only when everyone was asleep did she dare sneak out to the equipment shed to see the alien.

EIGHT

Talon still wasn't sure what to make of Ruru. She'd talked and talked and talked, before she'd curled up under his wing and gone to sleep. How she could keep so much information in her head…his head was almost spinning at all the things she'd said. The experimental crops they'd been growing here at Star Farm, simulating the conditions on Elysium so that when they had a successful harvest, they could simply replicate the system here on the planet's surface. Soil types, nutrient regimens, watering frequency, even the time of day they planted and harvested…not to mention companion crops and crop rotation. His head hurt, like that time he'd walked into one of the postgraduate lectures during his first year at university and the rapid fire information the lecturer had laid down had threatened to make his head explode. Ruru might look like a teenager, but she sounded like the Professor of Elysian Agriculture. He'd always liked smart girls, but this one…stars, he was glad he was in griffon form. Much easier to hide the raging boner he had for her.

Now, if only she wasn't curled up against his side, a warm weight beneath his wings, maybe he'd be able to think of unsexy things so he'd stop aching.

Tenebris came to the rescue, with no less than three dead rats hanging from her claws. She dropped them on the shed floor with a disturbingly loud splat. Sure enough, she'd gutted at least one of them, resulting in the pool of blood now spreading around the rat corpses.

Yes, that would do it. Hard to feel randy when you were staring at disembowelled corpses. And the smell…

Talon looked up into the shadows, where he knew Tenebris the sooty quoll meowl lurked. All he could see were her face and her spots in the darkness, but he knew she was staring at him, a question in her expression.

Talon sighed. "Yes, good girl, you can have one for dinner."

Unlike the rest of his flock, which were mostly crosses between barn owls and tabby domestic cats, Tenebris and her sisters had been bred from a mix of sooty owl and spotted quoll DNA. As the oldest member of Generation 3, Tenebris was the first to be tested out in the field. When she was fully grown, she'd be bigger than the barn meowls, but her catch rate even as a juvenile, the same size as the other adult meowls, made her a formidable hunter.

She selected a rat, then proceeded to try and swallow it whole. For a moment, Talon thought she might choke on the enormous rodent, but then she gave a big gulp and all that he could see of the rat was the tail poking out of the meowl's beak, and the satisfied look on Tenebris's face. If her sisters were anywhere near as good as her at hunting, he'd be breeding up more sooty quoll owls next season.

What was it Ruru had said? Something about the advertising for the Colony. The bit about building a better world together. The advertising had shown all these pretty pictures of what the perfect future would look like, based on the actual interior of the Colony, to make people believe they could actually live in that better world. While the truth was that they wouldn't – their kids or grandkids would. Or Tenebris's grandkids would. Because just like

Ruru…it was too soon to be thinking about a future with kids in it, when he was barely finding his own feet here. He was way too young to be responsible for someone else right now. Well, except for the meowls. And the meowls mostly took care of themselves.

With a dip of her head and a prolonged blink in farewell, Tenebris spread her wings and headed back out into the night to continue hunting.

Talon sighed. He was naturally a night owl, by virtue of his very nature as an owl griffon, but the perpetual twilight in the Nyx Dome meant he could keep whatever hours he pleased. So if he were to lay his head down on the straw beside Ruru's and join her in sleep…

NINE

Smoke. Rue smelled smoke. Instinct dragged her out of bed and over to the window, where the sun was inexplicably rising in the west. Not the sun, her groggy brain told her, but an enormous blaze that burned the very skies. The fire that took everything from her.

She had to help them. Had to save

them. This time, she'd find a way, and everything would be different. Had to help them.

Something dug into her shoulder. She turned to tell whoever it was to keep their fingers to themselves, only to see talons.

Rue blinked. Talons the size of an emu's foot. Only there were four toes instead of three, and they were sharper than anything on an emu. A cassowary, maybe, but…

She looked up into the alien's concerned eyes and drew in a deep gasp. Air that smelled of hay and feathers instead of smoke.

A nightmare. The same one she'd had far too many times, ever since the night they'd died. Including the night they'd died, because she'd smelled the smoke and seen the weird western dawn even at the agricultural college, several towns away.

But the alien's eyes were still on her, demanding an explanation. She sighed. She'd told him plenty about herself already, and the other girls had told her she talked in her sleep when she had nightmares, so he'd probably heard enough to deserve the rest of the story.

Rue took a deep breath. "My parents died in a fire. It was a routine burnoff, which had mostly died down, but a strong, hot wind came in overnight, fanned the embers of what was left, and it swept through my family's farm while they were asleep, before there was time to evacuate or anything. Their remains were still in the house when the fire crews came through… I was at the agricultural college at the time, so I wasn't home. I was supposed to go home on the weekend to help with the harvest, but the fire wiped out everything. Even the cellars, and the vintage that they'd started bottling…there was nothing left but ash. The only good news was that they think the emus escaped. They didn't find any remains of the flock.

"Then the insurance company refused to pay any compensation, because they said the fire was caused by government negligence at the burnoff site, which was true, and by the time the government had even considered they'd owe some sort of compensation, the bank came calling about all the loans my parents had taken out on the farm, which would have been paid off with the missing harvest and the first batch of wine, but with no wine and no harvest, the bank took everything. The government still hadn't sorted its shit out by the time I graduated – the college funded a sort of scholarship to keep me on until then – and Franny had already signed up for the FarmStars program, so I figured it was worth a shot. No incompetent governments in space to start fires.

"The sustainable vineyard was my parents' dream, but somewhere along the line, it became mine, too. I'd hear about things at college, and when I came home, they'd actually listen and talk about trying them out. If it weren't for the fire, it would have worked, I'm sure of it. I thought it might work on Elysium, but everything we've tried here just isn't suited to the light from Altan. It's like their dream is doomed.

"You know what the worst part is? That I was going home that weekend, and Dad was going to take me down to the airstrip so I could take my first flying lesson with one of the fire spotting pilots. If I'd been up there, I might have seen it. I could have saved them…"

The alien nodded gravely, as if he understood every word. Well, he probably did.

"I'm sorry, I…" The tears came then, flooding out of her like a faulty sprinkler system.

When she could finally see again, all

she could see was feathers. The alien had wrapped his wings around her, in a warm, soft, feathery hug that was the closest she'd been to anyone since her parents died.

She wanted to stay there forever, safe with someone who cared, but she knew she couldn't. She should get back to the dorm, before anyone noticed she was missing.

As if reading her mind, the alien stepped back, releasing her. Then he shook himself, and sort of…beckoned, as he headed out of the hayshed. Then he stopped in the doorway, and looked back at her, before beckoning again with his…claw? Talon? Front forepaw?

The he opened his beak in what Rue thought might be a smile, his eyes sparkling with mischief, as he patted his own back, then pointed at her, before he flapped his wings once.

"You want me to climb on your back so you can take me flying?" Even as the words left her lips, she knew they sounded ridiculous. She wasn't supposed to be anywhere near this alien, let alone riding him.

Yet he nodded and gave another flap, looking at her expectantly now.

If anyone caught her…she'd be stuck in solitary for a week.

Then again, actually flying again…only this time with an alien…it'd be worth it.

To hell with worrying.

She hiked up the hem of her nightgown, and climbed onto the alien's back. He was as wide as a horse, and it had been years since she'd ridden bareback, but no horse had ever been this soft. The fur on the alien's back was long enough to weave her fingers through. She wanted to bury her face in it, like she used to with the cats back on the farm when she was a kid. But that was hardly the sort of thing one did on first contact with an alien.

So she forced herself to grip him with her knees, like he was one of the agistment horses from long ago, and placed her hands lightly on his withers. Or whatever you called that bit that went down from his neck to his shoulder, seeing as he wasn't a horse.

He gave another nod, before he began to run. His smooth, cheetah-like stride carried them out of the hayshed, toward the fencing around the first field. Only the gate was closed and they were going too fast for her to say anything before…

He leaped, carrying them over the gate. Just as they started to descend, his wings came up, and with one mighty downsweep, launched them high into the air.

Then Rue couldn't help but bury her face in his fur, because with a vertical takeoff like that, it was either keep close to his back or fall off, and she'd be damned if she fell off. Even if this was her first bareback ride in years.

And what a ride it was.

They skimmed over the fields, where Rue glimpsed the owls wheeling and diving as they hunted. The only sound she could hear was the wind rushing through her ears — a sound she hadn't heard since she'd left Earth, seeing as the ventilation systems in the Colony never blew more than a gentle breeze. But the speed the alien flew at generated its own air current, strong enough to blow her hair back.

Higher and higher they flew, until they were above the grow lights that simulated daylight in the dome, and if Rue stretched her arm up, she fancied she could touch the dome itself.

She reached out, and found the dome surface wasn't as smooth as she'd thought. Instead of plasglass or something else transparent, it was cold, reflective metal, dotted with tiny lights that she'd thought were stars in the night sky above.

Tears welled in her eyes. She couldn't even see the sky in here.

But she didn't need to, Rue told herself, blinking the tears away. This was an alien planet, under an alien sun, and she was riding a flying alien inside a city so high-tech she could scarcely have dreamed it back on Earth, but this was where she would make her parents' dream come true.

With the help of aliens just like this one, if she had to. Up here, it was all so clear. No matter how many nightmares plagued her sleep, in her waking hours she had a different dream in mind – a future where she might not have been able to save her parents, but she could preserve their memories, and turn it into a legacy that would endure for generations.

She leaned forward, throwing her arms around the alien's neck as they soared across the metal cave that was Star Farm. "Thank you," she whispered.

TEN

Even after she'd hugged him good night and rushed off into the dormitory where she slept, Talon could feel her on his back. Riding him. Stars, but her body had felt perfect, her thighs holding tight to him as her hands stroked his fur. Now, if she'd been naked and he'd been a man instead of a beast, they could have turned that ride into one to remember…

Talon shook his head. He was supposed to be working, not fantasising about wild, animal sex with the hot farm girl.

He should do things properly. Ask her on a date, take her to dinner and bring her gifts of some sort, talk to her…all the normal things people did before they jumped into bed together. Or rolled around in the hay.

If only he hadn't promised the old woman not to talk to any of the girls. Though Ruru was definitely a woman, not a girl…

He dozed until dawn threatened, then called the meowls in to take them home.

When he got back to Meowl Mews — what Fang and Claw had jokingly called his own property, on a different level of the Nyx Dome to Star Farm, and the name had stuck — he found a message from Claw, asking if he should bring anything for the Go night tonight.

It was his turn to host again? Stars, that had come around fast.

He spent most of the afternoon tidying up, then ordered some food to arrive about the same time his friends did.

Achilles had sent his apologies. Something about training for the next match in the Arena. Talon snorted. Achilles hadn't made it to more than one or two of their Go nights since arriving in the Colony — he rarely left the Arena Dome. Maybe they should make him host more often. The Arena had onsite catering, after all, so it was easier for him to source food for everyone, and it wasn't like he needed to hide his nature from the staff he worked with every day, because they surely already knew his secret.

So it would be just the three of them tonight. The vampire, the griffon and the bear. Or the dentist, the ratcatcher, and the baker.

He should ask Claw to bring some pastries. Maybe even some extra so he could take them to Ruru tomorrow…

When the others arrived, Talon was tired. Too tired to keep his mind on the game, or his friends, because his thoughts kept darting back to Ruru.

Before he knew it, Claw had beaten him, and Talon was left staring at the board, with no idea how it had happened.

There was only one pastry left, too. Talon grabbed it, considering whether it was enough to take to Ruru tomorrow. No, tomorrow it would be stale. He should buy a fresh box from Claw on his way to Star Farm. So he ate it instead.

"I'm going to a speed dating event on Friday night, and I want you both to come with me as my wingmen," Claw said.

"What?" Talon blurted out, nearly spitting out the last mouthful of pastry. He didn't want to go to some matchmaking thing, where he was supposed to flirt with girls who'd turn their noses up at him when they found out he was a griffon. A chimera, a shifter who turned into a mismatched beast instead of an ordinary animal.

Not like Ruru. She liked his griffon form. She really was the perfect woman for him. If only she saw him as a man and not just a beast.

Fang muttered something about fated mates, some sort of vampire myth. Talon snorted. There was no such thing as fated mates. You either got along, or you didn't, and got divorced. But Fang sounded like he really believed in the myth.

"Then you have to go along! What if your fated mate is waiting at the Agency for you?" Talon asked. There. Let Fang go with Claw, and he could go to Star Farm with the meowls and take Ruru flying again. Maybe even take the risk of trying to talk to her.

"Don't griffons mate for life, too? What if you have a fated mate, and she's going to be at this event?" Fang asked.

Talon didn't know what other griffons did. He'd never actually met one. Owls mated for life, like his parents had, but griffons were as much cat as they were owl, and tom cats were legendary for not picking one partner.

Claw patted the air. "Guys, guys! If either of you meet the love of your life, I will totally stand aside and excuse you from wingman duties for the night. Who knows what could happen at these things? I just need you both to go with me. I'll even pay for your tickets, food and drink. How's that?"

Talon perked up. "Is this the one they

do at Forge?" He'd heard amazing things about the chef there.

"No, it's at the First Shot Cantina. The dating agency that meets at Forge is run by cupids, and it's all about looking for love, not specifically matching Humans with Titans. This one's…more for people interested in breeding."

"So the food and drink will be shit, but the chances of getting laid are super high," Talon translated. Not his scene. He'd rather spend the evening with Ruru.

"For you, maybe. I'm still a vampire," Fang said.

Talon clapped him on the back. "Yeah, but you're a rich, hot vampire dentist. I'm sure Human girls really go for that." He reached for his bowl of pasta. It was still warm, so he figured he'd best finish it off before it got cold.

"So it's a deal, yes? All three of us, going speed dating at the First Shot Cantina next Friday night. I'll send you the time and other details to your tablets. Do not be late." Claw said, draining the last of his drink. "I have bread to knead, so it'll rise in time for tomorrow, and my pastries won't make themselves." With a final wave, he was gone.

"You have time for another drink, or are you leaving, too?" Talon asked, turning to Fang.

Fang checked the time. "I have all night to get home, and no more patients tonight. I could manage another drink, if you have the good stuff."

Talon grinned. "Well, what do you

know? I got my hands on a bottle of genuine Earth-brewed tequila from Eden this week, as thanks for my pest control services. All those years at university, studying animals, when my real talents were in telling the meowls what to do while I sit back and let them do all the work."

"Yeah, but that's only because you bred superior meowls in the first place, which you couldn't have done without those years of study. And the fact that you bred them in space on the *Titanic*, and invited us up for a Go night there the very same night Titania went mad and all hell broke lose, which saved all our lives and most of your breeding stock…"

Talon pulled the stopper out of the

bottle, then glugged the contents into two glasses. He raised his glass, and nodded for Fang to do the same. "To meowls, miracles and fate that loves us," he said. He didn't dare mention Ruru, but silently he added his hope that she might find it in her heart to love him.

"Meowls, miracles, and fate's favour," Fang agreed, draining his glass with a grimace.

Talon shook his head. The vampire just didn't appreciate tequila properly.

"So, any idea why Claw would want to go to some matchmaking event for breeders?" Talon asked.

Fang just shook his head. "Maybe he thinks his biological clock is ticking. Or maybe…maybe he's doing this as a favour for someone, too, and taking us along so he doesn't look suspicious. I mean, you'll draw all the attention, so no one will notice him or me."

Talon burst out laughing. "Yeah, right up until the Human girls realise griffon babies are born in a litter of at least three. Then they run screaming from me, too."

"Let's face it, we're all doomed to remain lifelong bachelors. Achilles, too."

"Well, yeah, but he's…you know."

Fang nodded. "Yeah. Makes griffon quintuplets sound easy."

"I was only a triplet, you know. There might not be more than three."

Fang stared into his empty glass. "That's three more kids than I'll ever have." He reached for the bottle and poured two more glasses of tequila. "To being lifelong bachelors," he said solemnly.

"To lonely old men," Talon said, but as he downed his drink, he vowed the only lonely old men would be Fang and Claw, because the next time he saw Ruru, he was going to ask her out, no matter what the old woman said.

ELEVEN

"Hurry up and get dressed, Rue, or you'll be late," Donna scolded.

Rue looked up from the table she'd been wiping. "What? I'm not going to this dating thing!"

Donna made an impatient sound. "Of course you are. Linnaea's not feeling well, so you'll have to take her place."

Linnaea was already pregnant and probably throwing up somewhere, Rue translated.

"But why do I need to go? I'm going to work out my ten year contract on the farm. I don't need to have any babies," Rue said.

"Don't be silly. Your contract said ten years and four children. You're older than the others, so you need to get started early. Building a better world means carrying the children who will carry on after you, remember," Donna said.

More of this propaganda shit they'd rammed down their throats during training back on Earth. Rue was pretty certain Donna didn't believe in it, either, but some of the girls had taken to it like a new religion. Besides, Rue knew better than to call it what it was — it would only land her in solitary. That might save her from the dating thing, but then she'd also miss seeing the alien when he returned.

"Run along and get dressed right now, because if you make everyone late, the moment you get home, I'll put you in solitary," Donna threatened.

Ugh. Solitary wasn't worth the risk if it meant she still had to go to this thing.

"Fine," Rue huffed, and dashed to the common room.

The other girls were already dressed in a selection of cocktail dresses that were nothing like the drab clothes they wore around the farm. Between the pretty dresses, the makeup and the excitement building in the air, Rue couldn't help but smile. She didn't mind dressing up occasionally. But as for sleeping with some guy she'd just met…no, she had no intention of doing that.

The only dress left in Rue's size was a simple little black dress. A little bit of sparkly detail, a skirt that covered her arse, and a neckline that didn't spill her boobs out. Not bad, she thought as she checked it out in the mirror.

"Here, let me do your makeup," Franny said. "We need to emphasise your eyes. They're your best asset." As opposed to her too-small mouth, which the boys at school had called her resting bitch face. Of course, at the agricultural college, it had been different – more boys than girls, and she hadn't grown up with any of those boys, so she'd gotten along with them fine. Perhaps a little too well, in some cases, but Rue hadn't regretted the occasional roll in the hay at the time. But she'd known those boys. Tonight would be different.

Within minutes, Franny had worked her magic, and Rue couldn't help but admire the result. Her eyes looked enormous.

"Right, let's do this," Rue said.

Franny smiled. "It'll be fun."

Then Donna started handing out drinks that she insisted would enhance their fertility – which wouldn't work without a dick in the mix, Rue promised herself as she chugged it down with the rest of them – and waved them out the door.

TWELVE

Rue stood at the back of the crowd, drink in hand, watching the men saunter into the pub. Most of them looked nervous and normal, though a few had a sort of swagger about them that made her want to steer well clear. She recognised the dickheads, all right.

Then…there were three men who

arrived together. Friends, by the look of things, the way they gave each other shit as they signed some sort of waiver that one of the bar staff insisted upon. Donna had probably dealt with all the contract terms for the FarmStars girls, as usual.

But these three…they didn't belong among the desperate and dateless who made up the majority of the patrons. The first one who entered cast his gaze about like a predator assessing the room for possible threats. When he found none, he smoothed down his expensive clothes and turned to his friends.

Rue wouldn't have picked him for an alien if it weren't for the glimpse of fangs when he opened his mouth to speak to his friends. Definitely not like the other alien she'd met.

The biggest of the three was a big bear of a man, burly without being fat. Even though he wore a loose shirt, she could still see the outline of muscles upon muscles beneath it. He could probably lift her up with one hand, and not even break a sweat. He probably had a massive cock to match – which one of the more sex-minded girls would appreciate. Rue decided to avoid him.

And the third one…screamed rich farm boy from all the way across the room. He wasn't dressed any differently to the bear, but he was leaner, dark-skinned in contrast to the fanged alien's fairness. He moved like a scarecrow, as if he still wasn't used to walking around. Overgrown farm boy. Just like the ones she'd gone to college with. He looked around, let out a deep sigh, like he didn't want to be there and had only come to support his friends, and headed to the bar.

Well, Rue knew which man she was going to spend the evening with. At least she and the farm boy would have something to talk about.

THIRTEEN

They might have arrived together, but the moment Fang and Claw saw the ladies on offer, they deserted Talon. Which was fine by him. It's not like he wanted to hook up with some random girl anyway. He wondered if the others would notice if he left early.

"Gentlemen, it's time to take your

seats. The ladies are waiting to meet you!" simpered the faun who'd greeted them at the door.

Definitely time to go. Maybe he still had time to swing back home and pick up the meowls, so he'd have an excuse to go to Star Farm to see Ruru.

That's when he saw her. Dark as a shadow, hidden among all these women with their sparkly bright dresses and skin on display. But her eyes were fixed on him, warm with welcome.

"Hello, farm boy. Come sit with me," she said, kicking out the chair across from her.

The perfect woman. Talon couldn't help but obey. How could he leave when she was here?

"Hello, Ruru," he said.

She blinked, then shook her head and turned her eyes back onto him again, as if drinking in his innermost desires. "Why did you call me that?"

Stars. She didn't recognise him. Without wings and claws and a beak…with clothes on. Talon racked his brain for an explanation that wouldn't sound stupid. Ah, he had it.

"Because where I come from, a ruru is a small owl with enormous dark eyes, so big it makes their mouth look small and pursed, all puckered up in disapproval…or like you want a kiss."

Stars, he'd like to kiss her. Starting with her lips, then trailing down her neck to the breasts hidden beneath her dress, all the way down to…

"I'm not here to seduce anyone. I

came as a favour to a friend," Ruru said, folding her arms across her chest.

Talon laughed. "That makes two of us. I'd have preferred to stay home with my flock than come here."

"See? I knew you were a farm boy. Takes a farm girl to know one." She tipped her drink to him, then took a sip. Her face screwed up with horror as she spat the mouthful back into the glass it had come from. "God, what is that swill?" She shoved the glass away.

Talon held out his. "This one's beer, or that's what the bartender said. I'll get you one, if you want."

She sniffed the glass carefully, then shook her head. "I'll be fine, thanks. So, what's your name, farm boy?"

She really didn't recognise him.

"Talon. I grew up on Tito, on my parents' fruit farm. Mangoes, mostly, though they grew other things."

"What was it like?" she asked, turning those big eyes on him.

"Miserable, mostly. Well, the mango part, anyway. When you're around them all the time, it's not long before you can't stand them. Oh, but the guavas. At harvest time, I could live off those. So sweet, and they smelled amazing. Better yet, my sisters didn't like them, so I never had to share. Then there were the rice fields. Full of frogs to keep the bugs down, and while we were allowed to catch them, we always had to put them back into the water. I remember this one time, I must have been about four, I caught this frog so big I could barely hold it…"

Talon's mouth just couldn't seem to stop babbling, while he stared into her eyes and she read the secrets of his soul.

She smiled, and nodded, and listened. When he tried to turn the conversation to her, she'd just shrug and say she wasn't all that interesting, then ask him another question, those eager eyes waiting to drink in his answer.

He talked about his sisters and his parents, and the farm back on Tito, which was overrun by robots now. His family had taken a farm in the Ag Dome, where they were busily growing an orchard to help supply the Colony. Well, mostly they supplied the high end restaurants for the moment, because there wasn't enough for everyone, but in another year or two, his sisters planned on opening up a grocers where they could sell their produce, like the Mer sold their fish in the city.

"There are merpeople here? Real mermpeople?" Her eyes grew impossibly wide.

"Of course. Where there are Titans, there are merpeople. They're sort of…peacekeepers…" Except for Allie, of course. The Mer enforcer was terrifying when she needed to be. He'd heard stories… Talon shook his head. He didn't want to scare Ruru. "My friend Achilles dated a Mer girl once. He said the sex was amazing, but she only wanted to do it in the water. He almost drowned one night that she wanted to be on top…" He trailed off, feeling his cheeks grow hot. He shouldn't be telling Ruru this.

"How is that even possible? I mean, aren't they just sort of scales and a tail below the waist?" Ruru asked, mystified.

Of course, she was Human. She'd never met a Mer.

"Only when they want to be. They're shifters. They can be aquatic, or they can look just like a Human, so you'd never know what they truly are." Like Allie, who passed for Human among Humans, though no Titan was stupid enough to make that mistake.

"Are all aliens shifters?"

It was on the tip of his tongue to tell her. Stars, he wanted to. He wanted to shift then and there and show her exactly what he looked like, so she'd know it was him.

But he should answer her question first. "No, not everyone. Titans come in all shapes and sizes and...sorts. There are shifters, but there are elementals who take care of the water supply and the ventilation ducts. Vampires like Fang, or dryads who live in trees, or angels, djinn, demons...even I don't know all the creatures Titans can be. It's not polite to ask, especially when there are new hybrids born all the time."

"Like the alien Human hybrids they're trying to conceive here?" she asked, nodding to the other tables. The other empty tables. There was almost no one else left in the bar but them and the bartender.

"I don't know about that. I thought

the Colony was offering the hybrid birth bonus to encourage interspecies relationships, and no relationship is closer than when you're getting naked with someone and making a baby…" Stars, he was blushing again. Thank the stars she couldn't see it.

"What bonus?"

How could she not have heard about it? She was here, like all the rest of them, hoping to cash in on it. Except she'd said she was here as a favour to her friend. But surely her friend had heard about it…it'd been on all the orientation stuff, and advertised all over the entertainment channels. Even the aircars had posters proclaiming it.

Talon opened his mouth.

"Last drinks before the bar closes. The

coupling capsules are open all night, so if you'd head into one, you might just have time for a quickie before midnight…" the bartender barked, his eyes crawling over Ruru.

"Where did the time go?" she murmured, rising. Instead of going toward the back of the Cantina where the other couples had gone, she headed for the front door.

"Wait, will I see you again?" he blurted out.

She bobbed her head. "I'll be here next time there's a speed dating event, I imagine. Nice talking to you," she said as she left.

FOURTEEN

"I'm sorry I wasn't here last night. I had to go to this speed dating event. One of my friends was sick and I had to take her place," Ruru said as she stepped into the hayshed. "You wouldn't believe all the things I didn't know about the Colony or about Titans that I learned while I was there. Like that's what your people are called, and while some of them are shapeshifters, there are all kinds of different abilities, but it's rude to ask, so no matter how much I'm dying to, I shouldn't or I'll offend people. And how this isn't the only farm in the Colony, and soon they'll produce enough food so we won't have to eat ration bars all the time. And the alcohol is ghastly, even the beer, because it's not brewed properly. Or at all. It's all chemical cocktails created to get people drunk, but nothing like the real thing. I bet there'll be a riot when the first wine vintage is bottled, because what they called wine in that pub smelled more like something that belonged in a urinal…"

She tucked herself in under his wing, and the other side of their conversation spilled out. The words she hadn't said in the pub, all the thoughts and feelings she'd had while he kept babbling about himself. But she'd listened to every word, actually listened, and she was even talking about how she'd have to go back next week, to help her friends find partners, and there was so much more she wanted to know. So much more she wanted to ask…

Every word she spoke only cemented the certainty growing in his heart. If there were fated mates, then Ruru was surely his, the most perfect woman he'd ever met, and the only one he wanted.

Not even a supermassive black hole could keep him away from meeting up with her at the Cantina next week.

It wasn't until she slid off the haybales

and wished him good night before dashing out into the darkness that he realised she still hadn't noticed that Talon the man and Talon the griffon were one and the same.

Next week, he'd tell her, he promised himself.

At least this way he could keep his agreement with the old woman and not talk to the girls on the farm – he'd already made a date with her at the Cantina to meet up again next week. And he couldn't wait.

FIFTEEN

"You're eager tonight," Claw said as they followed Fang into the Cantina. "I know he thinks he's found his fated mate, but you don't believe in those things, right?"

Talon thought of Ruru. "Maybe I'm beginning to believe. The right woman…could make me believe almost anything. Including that there's a fated mate for everyone out there."

Claw shook his head. "Not everyone. Just a rare, lucky few."

There she was. Sitting at the same table as last time, looking expectantly toward the door. Then she smiled, just for him, and waved.

"Well, I don't know about you, but I am definitely feeling lucky tonight," Talon said, striding through the pub patrons like they weren't there.

"Yeah, well, there's a week's worth of condoms in that box. Make sure you use them," Claw said, before he veered away. Probably to meet up with the girl who'd entranced him last week.

"I can't find her." Fang was suddenly in his way, a big white wall of worry. "She's not here."

"Who?" Talon asked. Ruru was here — she was the one who mattered. Not whoever Fang's conquest had been last week.

"Dandelion," Fang said, scanning the crowd like he expected to find her.

Talon snorted. "Dandelion? You believe your fated mate is some girl called Dandelion?"

"I don't know if she's my mate. But there's something about her…and I need to see her again…" And Fang was gone.

Talon shook his head. Vampires were weird, and Fang was weirder than most. But he was a good guy, with a good heart, so Talon hoped he found the girl, especially if she was his fated mate.

Speaking of fated mates…

"Ruru," he breathed as he sat across

from her.

She laughed. "Actually, it's just one Rue, not two, but when you say it like that, I have to admit, I could absolutely get used to it."

Talon raised his eyebrows. "Are you flirting with me? Because I thought last week you said you didn't intend to seduce anyone."

She blushed. "I'm not, but I enjoyed talking to you last week. So much that I was hoping I'd see you again today. You said something about the Central Intelligence on Tito, and how it was a big AI that sort of ran everything, and there were robots. I wondered what it might be like. Could you tell me?"

So he did. All the good things, the useful things, that the Central

Intelligence and its robot army had done for Tito and Alba to make everything run smoothly before the AI had gone mad and started killing people. Unlike most of the other survivors, he hadn't seen any of the attacks in person – just on the news. He and the others had been sleeping off a drunken Go night on the *Titanic* when everything went to shit on the surface.

A lot of those good things were here in the Colony, too. Universal health care and a basic income. Paid parental leave, and housing for everyone. Making sure everyone had access to the same opportunities, at least here in the Colony. On the other planets, which weren't terraformed, life could be harsher, but the people out there were the ones doing the terraforming, so that there could be other cities, just like this one, throughout the system.

Stars, they'd had it so good on Tito. It hadn't been perfect, but it had been close. Until the stupid AI had malfunctioned and wrecked everything they'd created.

Before he could stop himself, he was telling her the story of how the *Titanic* had gone from empty research lab to rapidly filling colony ship as the refugees arrived from all over the system. Without the *Titanic*, they all would have died.

"Is that how you all got here? Where is the *Titanic* now?" She let out a little laugh. "I'm sorry, there was a ship by that name on Earth that met with a bad end. I can't believe your people would name a ship that, but I suppose if you didn't know…"

He stared at her. How could she not know?

"Your people destroyed the *Titanic*. Hurled a huge ice asteroid into it and smashed it into bits, killing those aboard before they could even get to the escape pods. That's what started the war."

Her mouth dropped open. "That's horrible! I can scarcely believe…I mean, I knew there was a war and a peace treaty and we're all supposed to be sharing this system now, but I only heard about it when we woke up here. Donna definitely didn't tell us about that. I'm so sorry, Talon. Did you lose anyone you loved during the war?"

Talon shook his head. "Colleagues,

acquaintances…people I knew, or had gotten to know while we were on the ship, but my family spent most of the war on Delta, helping the terraformers. I believe they planted the first coconut trees on one of the islands there, and the last I heard, they hadn't died. The trees, I mean. My family are all in the Ag Dome here now." He had Fang to thank for that. While robots had been razing the cities, Fang had sent one of his ships down to collect his family and the food supplies that had proved invaluable during the voyage.

She gave him a sad smile. "It must be nice to have your family close, where you can visit them whenever you want."

Too late, he remembered that she'd lost her family in the most horrifying circumstances. He started to stammer out an apology.

"Where is she?"

The shout came from an angry looking bloke who held the bartender by the throat, his legs dangling a good metre above the ground. "Where is she?" he asked again.

"Mr Shade. If we could take this to my office…" the bartender choked out.

The angry man lowered the bartender so his feet touched the ground, before marching him out the back through a door marked STAFF ONLY.

"What kind of creature is he?" Ruru whispered.

"The angry one? Incubus. You can tell from his markings, which glow when he's feeding. They feed on emotion, incubi. So the more scared the other guy gets, the more powerful the incubus becomes. Not to be confused with a succubus, who feeds on sexual energy. The high from an orgasm. Most people believe that incubi are all men, and succubi are all women, but it's not true. I've heard that incubi are actually a sort of weak vampire hybrid, though I don't know what the other part of their heritage is, while succubi are something entirely different. In fact…"

"Where is she?"

The incubus was back, though there was no sign of the bartender, and now he was headed right for them.

Talon took a deep breath, ready to shift to protect Ruru. He didn't want to reveal himself like this, but if he had to…

"Where is she? All you girls are from that whore farm. Where's the blonde one who wore white last week?"

Talon could feel his anger rising. Feeding the incubus, no doubt, but that wouldn't matter when he tore the man's throat out with his talons.

Ruru's hand shot up to stop him. She took a deep breath, then said calmly, "I don't know who you mean. If you're looking for a particular girl from Star Farm, then you need to speak to Donna, the woman in charge of the farm. If anyone knows, it'll be her."

The incubus blinked, his markings fading as the anger drained out of him. "Thank you. I will." He stormed off.

Ruru let out a breath. "Actually, I

think he meant Dani. She was wearing a white dress last week, and she does have blonde hair. I heard she hooked up with a vampire last week. I wouldn't have believed it if you hadn't told me they actually existed. She's not here tonight. She stayed at the farm. Do you think maybe the vampire hurt her?"

The only vampire who'd been here last week was Fang. Who'd also been looking for someone. "Dandelion?" he asked, and Ruru nodded. "The vampire is my friend, and a dentist. He wouldn't have hurt her. I think he had a bit of a thing for her, actually." He didn't dare mention fated mates or other myths Ruru had probably never heard of. "I wouldn't have let the incubus hurt you, either. If he'd so much as laid a hand on you…"

She smiled. "Thanks. I should probably call it a night, though. It's getting late and I should probably warn Donna that an angry incubus called Mr Shade is looking for her."

"Will I see you again next week?" he burst out, not liking how desperate he sounded.

A faint blush coloured her cheeks. "Of course." And then she was gone.

SIXTEEN

Flora herded them all off to bed when they returned, so Rue didn't have a chance to talk to Donna. In fact, she barely saw or heard Donna at all over the next week, because they were so busy harvesting the corn. More than once, Rue wished for some of the robots they'd talked about in training. The same sort Talon had said helped out on his family's farm, back on Tito. Why weren't there any robots here? They'd had to do classes on robot maintenance, to make sure they could do basic repairs, and then there'd been the programming classes so they could tell the robots what to do.

Stuff she hadn't needed at all. Not for the first time, she wondered why things had turned out so different to what they'd been trained to expect on Earth. Maybe it was something to do with the war, or the aliens.

That might explain it.

"You! I've heard you think you're too good to bear a child for this Colony!"

Rue shook herself out of her reverie to find Donna standing in front of her, pointing at her.

"Me?" Rue asked weakly.

"The only reason you are attending this speed dating event is so that you can conceive a child for the Colony. It is a privilege to be allowed to socialise with the other colonists, but it is one that some of you don't deserve. So at the speed dating event tonight, I want to hear that every single one of you has taken a man to one of the coupling capsules tonight. Any girl who does not will find themselves in solitary tomorrow morning, where she will remain for the next month!"

Rue closed her eyes. She couldn't spend a week in a room with nothing to do, let alone a whole month. They had to get the harvest in, and then plant the new fields…

"Do you understand me?" Donna demanded.

"Yes," Rue whispered.

"Will you fuck a man tonight to fulfil your contractual requirements as a member of the FarmStars Collective?"

Rue squirmed. "Yes."

Donna held her gaze for an agonisingly long moment, before she released her. "That goes for all of you!"

Heads nodded.

"These are desperate men. It won't take long. Get it done, make it quick, and then come home to the farm."

"Yes, Donna," they chorused.

Over Rue's dead body, she thought but didn't say. She had to come up with a plan before tonight.

SEVENTEEN

This time when Talon sat down across from Ruru, her frown only deepened.

"What's wrong?" he asked.

She swallowed. "I don't know how to say this, but will you please come to one of the coupling capsules with me? I can explain in there." She glanced around, as if she expected someone to be watching her.

Talon bobbed his head. "Sure."

She took his hand and led him to the back of the pub, where both walls were filled with what looked like large lockers. She pressed her palm to the pad beside the nearest one and the door swung open. It was like a shower stall, only horizontal, with a thin mattress on the bottom. It would be a tight fit with two of them in there.

"Get in," she said.

Talon swallowed, but it made sense for him to climb in first. He was much bigger than she was. He slid in all the way, trying to squish up against one wall to give her as much space as possible. Until she slid inside, her body rubbing against his.

Then she closed the door and everything went dark.

"Shit, where's the light?"

A frantic search ensued, which mostly involved feeling around the walls and ceiling for a switch, but in such close quarters, it was impossible to avoid touching her or pressing against her in the confined space. So that by the time she found a light switch and managed to turn it on, he had the biggest hard on in the history of hard ons and no way he could shift into griffon form to hide it.

"I don't suppose you brought me in here to seduce me," he said, trying to make light of their situation. Of his situation. He'd turned himself sideways, back to the wall, to keep as much distance between them as possible. So he didn't poke her anywhere. Well, unless she wanted him to.

"I was told if I didn't take a man to a capsule tonight, I wouldn't be allowed to see you again. They'd lock me up," Ruru said.

"Who said that?" Whoever it was, Talon was going to set the meowls on them.

"I…it doesn't matter. What matters is that I did it, so I won't be in trouble now. We just have to stay in here long enough for them to believe we did it, and then we can go back to the pub."

"It does matter. No one should be forced to have sex with anyone they don't want to, or locked up for not doing it. That's illegal, Ruru."

She sighed. "Not if I signed a contract.

It's part of the conditions of me coming to the Colony. Of all of us girls at Star Farm. We have to…"

"No. You don't. You hear me, Ruru? You are your own woman. You don't have to do anything you don't want to." When she wouldn't meet his eyes, Talon slipped a hand under her cheek and gently turned her head to face him. "You don't have to do anything or anyone you don't want to."

Tears shimmered in her eyes. "I want…"

Talon wasn't entirely sure what happened. Whether he kissed her or she kissed him or they both sort of lunged and met in the middle, but his lips were on hers and by every star in the galaxy, he had no intention of stopping. Not while those big, dark eyes were filled with desire, begging him…

For what?

It didn't matter what. He'd give her anything. Everything.

Oh, stars. She was as wet for him as he was hard for her, and she wasn't wearing any underwear. All he had to do was free his cock and he could plunge deep into the heaven that was her body.

"Yes, yes," she moaned as his fingers brushed against her clit.

He wanted…no, needed…to hear her moan like that again. To moan his name like that.

Blindly, his fingers went to work on her. Rubbing, circling, teasing her until she was practically sobbing, begging him for release. When she screamed for joy, he almost came in his pants.

"More. I want more, Talon. Please," she begged, reaching for his cock so that he was under no illusions as to what she wanted.

But he knew what she wanted. She'd told him.

He pulled out the box of condoms Claw had given him, and struggled to put one on without being able to actually see.

"What are you doing?" she asked. "I want you inside me now, Talon. Please."

"Just putting a condom on. I know you don't want kids until you have that farm of your dreams. With the vineyard and the emus."

"Talon."

"There. It's on. I'm all ready for you, Ruru. Maybe you should lie on top of me, so you can ride me, but careful not to bump your head."

"Talon."

She wasn't moving. In fact, she'd tugged her skirt down, and pressed her thighs together, like she'd changed her mind.

"What's wrong?" he asked. Because whatever it was, he would fix it. For her.

"I never told you about the farm, or the emus."

"Sure you did. You had a really bad nightmare, about the night your parents died, and I woke you up, and then…" His voice died. She'd told his griffon that. Not Talon the man.

"Get out."

Wordlessly, he did what she told him. Then she climbed out, too, and looked down.

"Go to the bathrooms and deal with that before someone sees you and knows we didn't do it. And get rid of that thing, too. We're not supposed to use birth control if we're trying for a baby." She shoved him in the direction of the bathrooms.

He'd never jacked off so fast in his life, but by the time he headed back to the pub, she was gone.

Talon swore.

EIGHTEEN

Rue saw the alien and his crew arrive, but it took every bit of her willpower not to follow him out to the hayshed. She wanted to throw him to the ground and have her way with him. She wanted to shout at him for deceiving her and not telling her who he was. She wanted to slap herself for being so stupid and not realising the two aliens she liked were the same man. She wanted to beg him to take her flying again. And she also never wanted to see him again, so she wouldn't be reminded about how stupid she'd been.

"Where is she?"

Rue would recognise that voice anywhere. It was Mr Shade the incubus, only instead of shouting at the bartender, now he was shouting at Donna.

Rue tiptoed across the dining room, and peeked through the door to Donna's office, so she might hear the conversation better.

"She's not here, Mr Shade. Her contract has already been sold. You've been outbid, and that's that. She belongs to someone else now."

"She can't be the only blonde you have. I don't care which one — you promised me a blonde virgin, so by the stars, you will give me a blonde virgin, or I will…"

"You will what, Mr Shade? Go to the Watch and tell them that you tried to buy a child to be your sex slave? Please do."

That whore farm. Was that what he'd meant? That Donna sold girls as sex slaves to men with enough money to pay for them? Who had she already sold? Was it Dani?

"You will sell me one of your girls, or I will go to the Watch and tell them you have already sold one. It was to that vampire, wasn't it? He'll probably suck her dry within the week, and when she turns up, I'll go to the Watch with information…"

"Very well. Return in the morning, and in the meantime, I will prepare the necessary contracts, while you make sure you have the money to pay for them."

Rue raced outside before Donna could catch her eavesdropping. Only…where to run to now? The other girls surely wouldn't believe her.

But Talon might. He'd seen and heard Mr Shade.

Rue hurried to the hayshed, hoping he'd be there.

Only…he was.

NINETEEN

She'd expected fur and feathers, loafing on the haybales like a giant cat. Not…holy hell on a sexy stick. One she really, really wanted to ride…

He lay on the haybales all right. Spreadeagled like one of those medieval pictures of the perfect man, only those pictures hadn't included enormous spotted wings. Or a cock that jutted out quite that much. Or….

"You love my tail. Even if you hate the rest of me, tell me you still love my tail."

Big and soft and spotted and fluffy and almost as long as she was tall. She couldn't lie. "I do love your tail. It's the part where you're him and he's you and I don't know what to think any more."

He sat up and held out his hands. "I'm a shifter, Ruru. An owl griffon shifter. I can transform from almost Human right into the flying beast you first met. I think I fell in love with you that very first night, when you came to me in the middle of the night and fell asleep wrapped in my wings. I'd been trying to work up the courage to ask you out on a date when I saw you at the Cantina, and I wanted to tell you, but I wasn't sure how. I want to ask you to give me another chance, but I'm not even sure if I deserve one. And you…you're so beautiful and talented and dedicated and driven, and I'm just a chimera pest control man with a strange biological quirk that lets me talk to meowls. I don't deserve you."

Tears sprang to her eyes. "I'm just a stupid farm girl who lost her family in a fire and couldn't even put two and two together to realise the alien I'd fallen for here on the farm, who I wished was a man, was the same man I'd been talking to at the pub!"

"You're not stupid. You know more about farming than any of my professors at college back on Alba."

"But I didn't think it was even possible that a white owl griffon with silver spots could possibly be the black farm boy helping his friend. I just…"

"Can you forgive me?"

One look at him, and she couldn't say no. She wanted to climb into his lap and ride him to the very stars above.

She wet her lips. "That depends. Do you have any condoms left?"

He shook the box. "A week's worth, I believe."

She tore off her dress, not caring where it landed, them shimmied out of her underwear. Then she climbed into his lap while he hurried to roll on a condom before she sank down on his length, moaning with delight as he filled her.

His wings closed around her, holding her close, as she rode him, tentatively at first, then harder as they found a rhythm together, moving as one as she felt her climax building, until she could no longer hold back the scream rising from her throat…

That's when he kissed her, devouring her mouth and swallowing her screams as simultaneous orgasms rocked them both.

He caught his breath first. "Are you all right? Did I hurt you?"

Rue laughed softly. "I'm fine. More than fine. You gave me exactly what I wanted. Like our bodies were made for each other. I want to do that all over again, all night if we can, every night.

If…if you want to, that is."

"I want to hear you moan and scream my name over and over, all night. Not here, where we might wake someone, and not in one of those coffin capsules, where there's no space for anything. I want to take you home, Ruru, and lie you down on my bed so we can make love all night, and maybe all day, too."

"Yes," she whispered.

"In the meantime, we should get cleaned up, and you should get some sleep."

Every part of her wanted to stay here, cradled in his lap with his cock deep inside her, but she knew he was right. She did need sleep.

The cleanup was quick, with cold water from the tap in the shed, and no one seemed to notice when she joined the other girls trooping out of the common room to the dormitory. She was the last to brush her teeth, so everyone else was already in bed as she reached for the switch to turn out the lights.

No, not everyone. Two beds were empty. Dani's…and Iva's. The two blonde girls.

Rue's heart sank. She'd been so preoccupied with Talon that she'd forgotten all about the danger, and Donna.

She flicked off the light, then hurried back to the bathroom. "Forgot to floss," she mumbled in case anyone cared.

Only instead of heading out to the bathhouse, she made for the hayshed instead.

"You should be in bed," Talon chided.

"No. It's not safe here. Two of the girls are missing. I think…I think Donna sold them as sex slaves. To that angry Mr Shade, and possibly to your vampire friend."

Talon shook his head. "Not Fang. He'd never do something like that. He was looking for the same girl as the incubus, remember. It must be some other vampire."

"I need to ask Donna to tell me the truth." Even though Donna held her contract, could send her to solitary forever, or sell her like might have happened to Iva and Dani.

"I'm coming with you." In an instant, he was at her side – not the man, but the very deadly looking griffon.

But Donna wasn't in her office, or her cottage, where the mess inside told them something bad had happened there, but they didn't know what.

"It's not safe here. I'm taking you home," Talon said.

"But we're not supposed to leave the farm without Donna's permission," Rue said. If Donna had only left to run an errand, and came back to find her gone…she'd be in deep shit. Solitary would be just the start.

"She's not here to give it, and by the look of this place, she left in a hurry, so she'd not likely to be back. You'll be safe at my place. I'll smuggle you out under my wings. The meowls will perch on top and hide you."

Rue closed her eyes. "All right."

TWENTY

The meowls flew off into the dark reaches of Meowl Mews, before Rue slowly climbed down from Talon's back. "This is all yours?" she asked. "It's as big as Star Farm."

He shrugged. "The meowls need space. Eden keeps offering me all sorts of crops and livestock to fill it up with, but I don't need any of that. This place is for the meowls."

"And you."

"And us." He had a crazy thought. "You said you wanted a farm of your own, to try things out. Try them here. As long as none of the plants or livestock endangers the meowls, you can put in whatever you want."

"Truly?" Even in the dim light of the Nyx Dome, her eyes shone.

"It's all yours."

"Thank you!" She hugged him.

He shifted back into a man before he hugged her back, then scooped her up into his arms to take her into the house. "In the morning, we can go over the surveillance footage for Star Farm, and try to find out what happened to Donna, and to your friends."

"You can do that?"

Talon grinned. "Pest control officers need to be able to see everything. So I have access to every camera in the Colony, just in case I need it."

"Are there cameras in here?"

"Not in the house. Which is a good thing, because I intend to take you to bed properly this time, just you and me, with no one, not even Lothario the meowl, watching." Pervy little meowl. He'd seen his eyes glittering from the rafters above just as Ruru had sat in his lap, and then of course Talon had forgotten all about the randy little bastard.

Now, though…

He carried Rue through the house to

his bedroom, where he tossed her on the bed. The proper, griffon sized bed dwarfed her, but she looked so perfect there…

"Every time I've pictured you here, it always starts off gentle and slow, but then we get going and it turns into wild, crazy, griffon sex," he admitted.

She sat up, pulling her nightdress over her head. Her underwear followed it onto the floor. "I like the sound of wild, crazy griffon sex," she said.

"It'll go on for hours. You'll have more orgasms than you can count," he warned her.

"What are you waiting for, then?"

He grinned. "For you to get into position. On your hands and knees, right up at the head of the bed."

Stars, she looked beautiful like that. Like everything he'd ever wanted in a woman.

He needed wings for this, and claws. Plus a tail to play with.

He entered her slowly, pushing in deep until she'd taken his entire length. Only then did he run his hands up her belly and breasts, pulling her flush against his chest. "Put your hands on the headboard, and hold on," he whispered in her ear.

She did as he asked, rising up as she tightened around him. Stars, she felt good.

He wrapped her in his wings, until he could feel her breasts pressed against his feathers. Then he fastened his hands around her hips.

DEMELZA CARLTON

TWENTY-ONE

What was he waiting for?

"Are you sure you're ready for this?" Talon whispered in her ear. "Tell me if you want me to stop."

She wanted to tell him to just start already, because she knew there was no way she wanted to stop, but wild alien griffon sex was new to her. Who knew what it might involve?

So she just nodded, then felt something soft stroke down her belly, until it pressed against her clit. Tickling, rubbing, faster and faster until…

"Oh my God, that's your tail? That's…Talon…oh!"

Her orgasm hit, and she clenched down on him as she came hard.

That's when he began to fuck her. This was nothing like the gentle thrusts as she'd sat in his lap earlier. No, now he pounded into her, rough and hard and deep so that it was all she could do to cling to the headboard with white knuckled hands as his cock rubbed every bit of her insides, and his tail tickled her clit and his wings…oh God his wings…she'd heard of people using feathers in bed, but this was a hundred feathers, all over her breasts and her nipples and her belly, sliding over her as every thrust shook her body. And she loved every moment of it, as the orgasms began to come in waves.

"Talon!"

"Oh my God, Talon!"

"OH, TALON!"

"God, Talon!"

"Oh, Talon, oh!"

Too many orgasms to count, but she didn't want him to stop. To ever stop.

His breath was hot on the back of her neck as he pounded into her in a frenzy.

Oh God, she was close, and this orgasm felt like it was going to be bigger than the rest. Bigger and stronger and…oh God…

She screamed until she ran out of breath, then screamed again. She barely heard Talon roaring her name as he came with her, just as hard. A slight sting at the base of her throat, where she realised he'd bitten her. Marked her. Yet that felt right, too.

She was dimly aware of him prying her hands off his headboard, as he drew her down onto the bed, spooning in his arms.

"Too much for you, my little Ruru?" he asked as he withdrew from her.

She wanted to cry at the emptiness. "Never. I want more."

"Good. Because you remember how on the night we met, you said you loved my tail?"

Softness stroked her clit, sliding over it

and then inside her. Almost as thick as his cock, and longer, too.

"I want to make you love it even more."

He was fucking her with his tail, and she was about to…no, surely she couldn't…

"Oh my God, Talon!"

TWENTY-TWO

He pleasured Ruru with his tail far longer than he should have, for his cock was well and truly hard again and ready for her by the time he could bring himself to take his focus off her long enough to hunt for the box of condoms.

There they were.

She lay on her back now, gazing up at

him adoringly as he rolled on a fresh condom. One more time, and then they both needed some sleep. He was pretty sure it was tomorrow already, but he didn't care. He deserved a day off, and Ruru deserved everything her heart desired.

His comm chimed with an incoming call.

Talon ignored it and positioned himself between Ruru's legs. Then he lifted her legs over his shoulders and thrust. Slow and deep and gentle this time, to give her the sort of planet-shattering orgasm that shook her to her core.

Claw's voice rose from the comm. Must have been on autoanswer still from when he was in griffon form. "Stars take it, Talon, I know you're there. This won't wait until you wake up. I need you to get out of Star Farm immediately, do you hear me? Pack up your birds and go. Don't have any more contact with anyone from Star Farm. Especially not the girls."

Ruru stared up at him, wide-eyed. Talon leaned down and kissed her, not breaking his rhythm for a moment. Claw could take his stupid warnings and yeet them into a black hole. He was going to give his gorgeous girl one more orgasm before they went to sleep.

"Look, Talon, there's a reason those girls are isolated at Star Farm. Why they're not supposed to leave. Because if they get out and mix with the general population…the peace treaty, and everything we've built here in the Colony will be put at risk."

Ruru whimpered. She was close now, he could feel it. A few more strokes…

He reached over and ended the call.

And came hard to the blissfully sweet music of Ruru screaming his name.

In another part of the Nyx Dome, Claw finished his warning, not realising that Talon had already ended the call: "If just one of those girls gets out...she could start another war faster than the ice asteroid that destroyed the *Titanic*."

ABOUT THE AUTHOR

Demelza Carlton has always loved the ocean, but on her first snorkelling trip she found she was afraid of fish.

She has since swum with sea lions, sharks and sea cucumbers and stood on spray drenched cliffs over a seething sea as a seven-metre cyclonic swell surged in, shattering a shipwreck below.

Demelza now lives in Perth, Western Australia, the shark attack capital of the world.

The *Ocean's Gift* series was her first foray into fiction, followed by her suspense thriller *Nightmares* trilogy. She swears the *Mel Goes to Hell* series ambushed her on a crowded train and wouldn't leave her alone.

Want to know more? You can follow Demelza on Facebook, Twitter, YouTube or her website, Demelza Carlton's Place at:

www.demelzacarlton.com

More Books by Demelza Carlton

<u>**Colony: Aqua series**</u>

Halcyon (#1)

Poseidon (#2)

Apollo (#3)

<u>**Nightmares Trilogy**</u>

Nightmares of Caitlin Lockyer (#1)

Necessary Evil of Nathan Miller (#2)

Afterlife of Alana Miller (#3)

<u>**Mel Goes to Hell series**</u>

The Devil's Work (#1)

See You in Hell (#2)

Mel Goes to Hell (#3)

To Hell and Back (#4)

The Holiday From Hell (#5)

All Hell Breaks Loose (#6)

The Devil Goes to Heaven (#7)

<u>**Romance Island Resort series**</u>

Maid for the Rock Star (#1)

The Rock Star's Email Order Bride (#2)

The Rock Star's Virginity (#3)

The Rock Star and the Billionaire (#4)

The Rock Star Wants A Wife (#5)

The Rock Star's Wedding (#6)

Maid for the South Pole (#7)

<u>Romance a Medieval Fairytale series</u>

Enchant: Beauty and the Beast Retold

Dance: Cinderella Retold

Fly: Goose Girl Retold

Revel: Twelve Dancing Princesses
Retold

Silence: Little Mermaid Retold

Awaken: Sleeping Beauty Retold

Embellish: Brave Little Tailor Retold

Appease: Princess and the Pea Retold

Blow: Three Little Pigs Retold

Return: Hansel and Gretel Retold

Wish: Aladdin Retold

Melt: Snow Queen Retold

Spin: Rumpelstiltskin Retold

Kiss: Frog Prince Retold

Reflect: Snow White Retold

Roar: Goldilocks Retold

Cobble: Elves and the Shoemaker Retold

Float: Enchanted Horse Retold

Steal: Forty Thieves Retold

Call: Pied Piper Retold

Fall: Scheherazade Retold

Feather: Swan Maidens Retold

Cross: Billy Goats Gruff Retold

Weave: Rapunzel Retold

Claim: Puss in Boots Retold

Curse: Rose Red Retold

Cross: Three Billy Goats Gruff Retold

Weave: Rapunzel Retold

Claim: Puss in Boots Retold

<u>**Heart of Stone series**</u>

Heart of Steel (#0)

Broken Chains (#1)

Broken Bonds (#2)

Broken Dreams (#3)

www.ingramcontent.com/pod-product-compliance
Lightning Source LLC
Chambersburg PA
CBHW070957180726
48291CB00004B/1335